William Whitehead

The School for Lovers

A comedy. As it is acted at the Theatre Royal in Drury-Lane

William Whitehead

The School for Lovers
A comedy. As it is acted at the Theatre Royal in Drury-Lane

ISBN/EAN: 9783337064754

Printed in Europe, USA, Canada, Australia, Japan

Cover: Foto ©Andreas Hilbeck / pixelio.de

More available books at **www.hansebooks.com**

THE
School for Lovers,
A
COMEDY.

As it is Acted at the

THEATRE ROYAL in *Drury-Lane.*

By WILLIAM WHITEHEAD, Esq;
POET LAUREAT.

LONDON:

Printed for R. and J. DODSLEY in *Pall-mall*;
and Sold by J. HINXMAN, in *Pater-noster-row.*
MDCCLXII.

[Price One Shilling and Six-pence.]

ADVERTISEMENT.

THE following Comedy is formed on a plan of Monfieur de Fontenelle's, never intended for the ftage, and printed in the eighth volume of his works, under the title of Le Teftament.

The fcene of that piece is laid in Greece, and the embarraffing circumftances depend on fome peculiarities in the cuftoms of that country. Slaves likewife, as is ufual in the Grecian Comedy, act as confidantes to the principal perfonages. The Author, therefore, hopes he may be excufed for having made the ftory Englifh, and his own; for having introduced a new character, and endeavoured to heighten thofe he found already fketched out. The delicacy of the fentiments in Philonoe and Eudamidas, he has inviolably adhered to, wherever he could infert them properly, in his Cælia and Sir John Dorilant; and would willingly flatter himfelf, that he has made great and not contemptible additions to their characters, as well as to the others.

Thofe who will give themfelves the trouble to read both pieces, will fee where the Author is, or is not indebted to that elegant French Writer.

TO

THE MEMORY OF

MONSIEUR DE FONTENELLE,

THIS COMEDY IS INSCRIBED

BY A LOVER OF SIMPLICITY,

THE AUTHOR.

PROLOGUE.

As it was intended to have been SPOKEN.

SUCCESS makes people vain.—The maxim's true,
   We all confess it —— and not over new.
The veriest clown who stumps along the streets,
And doffs his hat to each grave cit he meets,
Some twelvemonths hence, bedaub'd with livery lace,
Shall thrust his saucy flambeau in your face.
Not so our Bard: tho' twice your kind applause
Has, on this fickle spot, espous'd his cause:
He owns, with gratitude, th' obliging debt,
Has twice been favour'd, and is modest yet.
Plain Tragedy, his first adventurous care,
Spoke to your hearts, and found an echo there.
Plain Comedy to-night, with strokes refin'd,
Would catch the coyest features of the mind:
Would play politely with your hopes and fears,
And sometimes smiles provoke, and sometimes tears.

   Your giant wits, like those of old, may climb
Olympus high, and step o'er space and time;
May stride with seven-leagu'd boots, from shore to shore,
And, nobly by transgressing, charm you more.
Alas! our Author dares not laugh at schools,
Plain sense confines his humbler Muse to rules.
Form'd on the classic scale his structures rise,
He shifts no scenes to dazzle and surprize.
In one poor garden's solitary grove,
Like the primeval pair, his lovers rove.
And in due time will each transaction pass,
—— Unless some hasty critic shakes the glass.

SUCCESS makes people vain.—The maxim's true.—
We all confess it—and not over new.
The veriest clown, who stumps along the streets,
And doffs his hat to each grave cit he meets,
Some twelvemonths hence, bedaub'd with livery lace,
Shall thrust his saucy flambeau in your face:

Not so our Bard—though twice your kind applause
Has, on this fickle spot, espous'd his cause:
He owns, with gratitude, th' obliging debt;
Has twice been favour'd, and is modest yet.

Your giant wits, like those of old, may climb
Olympus high, and step o'er space and time;
May stride, with seven-leagu'd boots, from shore to
        shore,
And, nobly by transgressing, charm ye more.
Alas! our Author dares not laugh at schools —
Plain sense confines his humbler Muse to rules:
He shifts no scenes—But here I stop'd him short ——
Not change your scenes? said I,—I'm sorry for't!
My constant friends above, around, below,
Have English tastes, and love both change and show:
Without such aids, even Shakespear would be flat—
Our crouded Pantomimes are proofs of that.
What eager transport stares from every eye,
When pullies rattle, and our Genii fly!

                                        When

P R O L O G U E,

When tin cascades like falling waters gleam :
Or through the canvas—bursts the real stream :
While thirsty Islington laments in vain
Half her New-River roll'd to Drury-Lane.

   Lord, Sir, said I, for gallery, boxes, pit,
I'll back my Harlequin against your wit ————
Yet still the Author, anxious for his play,
Shook his wise head —— What will the critics say ?
As usual, Sir — abuse you all they can ! —
And what the ladies —— He's a charming man !
A charming piece ! — One scarce knows what it means ;
But that's no matter ———— where there's such sweet
    scenes !
Still he persists — and let him — entre nous —
I know your tastes, and will indulge 'em too.
Change you shall have ; so set your hearts at ease :
Write as he will, we'll act it as you please.

PERSONS

PERSONS Represented.

Sir JOHN DORILANT, a Man of nice Honour, Guardian to Cælia,   } Mr. GARRICK.

MODELY, } Men of the Town,   { Mr. PALMER.
BELMOUR, }   { Mr. OBRIEN.

An old Steward to Sir John Dorilant,   Mr. CASTLE.

Footman to Sir John Dorilant,   Mr. FOX.

Lady BEVERLEY, a Widow Lady, Mother to Cælia,   } Mrs. CLIVE.

CÆLIA, Daughter to Lady Beverley, and Ward to Sir John,   } Mrs. CIBBER.

ARAMINTA, Sister to Sir John Dorilant,   } Mrs. YATES.

SCENE a Garden belonging to Sir John Dorilant's House in the Country, with an Arbour, Garden Chairs, &c.

THE

School for LOVERS.

✦ ⊹⊹⊹⊹⊹⊹⊹⊹⊹⊹⊹⊹⊹⊹⊹⊹⊹⊹⊹⊹⊹⊹⊹⊹⊹⊹⊹⊹⊹⊹⊹⊹⊹⊹⊹⊹ ✦

ACT I.

SCENE *the Garden.*

Enter ARAMINTA *with an affected Careless-ness, and knotting,* MODELY *following.*

MODELY.

BUT madam!

ARAMINTA.

But Sir! what can poffibly have alarmed you thus? You fee me quite unconcerned. I only tell you in a plain fimple narrative manner —— (this plaguy thread) —— and merely by way of conver-fation, that you are in love with Cælia; and where is the mighty harm in all this?

MODELY.

The harm in it, madam! have I not told you a

B   thou-

thousand and a thousand times that you were the
only woman who could possibly make me happy?

ARAMINTA.

Why aye, to be sure you have, and sworn a
thousand and a thousand oaths to confirm that af-
sertion.

MODELY.

And am not I here now expressly to marry you?

ARAMINTA.

Why that *too* is true — — but — — you are in love
with Cælia.

MODELY.

Blefs me, madam, what can I say to you? If it
had not been for my attendance upon you, I had
never known Cælia or her mother either, though
they are both my relations. The mother has since
indeed put some kind of confidence in me; she is a
widow you know——

ARAMINTA.

And wants confolation! The poor orphan too her
daughter! Well, charity is an excellent virtue. I
never confidered it in that light before. You are
vaftly charitable, Mr. Modely.

MODELY.

It is impoffible to talk with you. ——If you will
not do me juftice, do it to yourfelf at leaft. Is
there any comparifon betwixt you and Cælia?
Could any man of fenfe hefitate a moment? She
has yet no character. One does not know what
fhe is, or what fhe will be; a chit, a green girl
of fourteen or fifteen.

ARAMINTA.

Seventeen at leaft.—(I cannot undo this knot.)—

MODELY.

Well, let her be feventeen. Would any man of

3 .   judg-

judgment attach himfelf to a girl of that age? O'
my foul, if one was to make love to her, fhe
would hardly underftand what one meant.

A R A M I N T A.

Girls are not quite fo ignorant as you may imagine, Mr. Modely; Cælia will underftand you,
take my word for it, and does underftand you.
As to your men of judgment and fenfe, here is my
brother now; I take him to be full as reafonable as
yourfelf, and fomewhat older; and yet with all
his philofophy, he has brought himfelf to a determination at laft, to fulfill the father's will, and
marry this green girl. I am forry to tell you fo,
Mr. Modely, but he will certainly marry her.

M O D E L Y.

Let him marry her. I fhould perhaps do it myfelf, if I was in his place. He was an intimate
friend of her father's. She is a great fortune, and
was given to him by will. But do you imagine,
my dear Araminta, that if he was left to his own
choice, without any bias, he would not rather
have a woman nearer his own years? He might almoft be her father.

A R A M I N T A

That is true. But you will find it difficult to
perfuade me, that youth in a woman is fo infur-
mountable an objection. I fancy, Mr. Modely, it
may be got over. Suppofe I leave you to think of
it.—(I cannot get this right.)——   [Going.

M O D E L Y.

Stay, dear Araminta, why will you plague me
thus? Your own charms, my earneftnefs, might
prove to you ——

A R A M I N T A.

I tell you I don't want proofs.

MODE-

MODELY.

Well, well, you shall have none then. But give me leave to hope, since you have done me the honour to be a little uneasy on my account——

ARAMINTA.

Uneasy !——I uneasy !—— What does the man mean ? I was a little concerned indeed to give you uneasiness by informing you of my brother's intended marriage with Cælia. But——(this shuttle bends so abominably.)

MODELY.

Thou perplexing tyrant ! Nay, you shall not go.——May I continue to adore you! you must not forbid me that.

ARAMINTA.

For my part I neither command nor forbid any thing. Only this I would have you remember, I have quick eyes. Your servant.——(I wish this knotting had never come in fashion.)

[Exit Araminta.

MODELY.

Quick eyes indeed ! I thought my cunning here had been a master-piece. The girl cannot have told sure ! and the mother is entirely on my side. They certainly were those inquisitive eyes she speaks of, which have found out this secret. Well, I must be more cautious for the future, and act the lover to Araminta ten times stronger than ever. One would not give her up till one was sure of succeeding in the other place.

Enter BELMOUR *from behind with a Book in his Hand.*

BELMOUR.

Ha! ha! ha! well said Modely !

MODE-

MODELY (*ſtarting.*)

Belmour! how the duce came you here?

BELMOUR.

How came I here? —— How came you here—if you come to that? A man can't retire from the noiſe and buſtle of the world, to admire the beauties of the ſpring, and read paſtoral in an arbour, but impertinent lovers muſt diſturb his meditations.—Thou art the erranteſt hypocrite, Modely ——

[*Throwing away the book.*

MODELY.

Hypocrite!——My dear friend, we men of gallantry muſt be ſo.——But have a care, we may have other liſteners for aught I know, who may not be ſo proper for confidantes. [*Looking about.*

BELMOUR.

You may be eaſy on that head. We have the garden to ourſelves. The widow and her daughter are juſt gone in, and Sir John is buſy with his ſteward.

MODELY.

The widow, and her daughter! Why, were they in the garden?

BELMOUR.

They juſt came into it, but upon ſeeing you and Araminta together, they turned back again.

MODELY.

On ſeeing me and Araminta? I hope I have no jealouſies there too. However I am glad Cælia knows I am in the garden, becauſe it may probably induce her to fall in my way, by chance you know, and give me an opportunity of talking to her.

BELMOUR.

Do you think ſhe likes you?

MODE-

MODELY.

She does not know what she does.

BELMOUR.

Do you like her?

MODELY.

Why faith, I think I do.

BELMOUR.

Why then do you pursue your affair with Araminta? and not find some honourable means of breaking off with her?

MODELY.

That might not be quite so expedient. I think Araminta the finest woman, and Cælia the prettiest girl I know. Now they are both good fortunes, and one of them **I am** resolved to have, but which ———

BELMOUR.

Your great wisdom has not yet determined. Thou art undoubtedly the vainest fellow living—— I thought you brought **me down** here now to your wedding?

MODELY.

'Egad I thought so too, but **this** plaguy little rustic has disconcerted all my schemes. Sir John, you know, by her father's will, may marry her if he pleases, and she forfeits her estate if she marries any one else. Now I am contriving to bring it about, that I may get her, and her fortune too.

BELMOUR.

A very likely business, truly. So you modestly expect that Sir John Dorilant should give up his mistress, and then throw her fortune into the bargain, as an additional reward to the obliging man who has seduced her from him.

MODE-

MODELY.

Hum! why I don't expect quite that. But you know, Belmour, he is a man of honour, and would not force her inclinations tho' he loved her to distraction. —— Come, come, he is quite a different creature from what you and I are.

BELMOUR.

Speak for yourfelf, good Sir; yet why fhould you imagine that her inclinations are not as likely to fix upon him **as you? He** has a good perfon, **and is** fcarce older than yourfelf.

MODELY.

That fhews your ignorance; I am ten years younger than he is. My drefs and the company I keep, give a youth and vivacity to me, which he muft always want. An't I a man of the town? O that town, Belmour! Could I but have met thefe **ladies** there, I **had** done the bufinefs.

BELMOUR.

Were they never there?

MODELY.

Never.——Sir Harry Beverley, the father of this girl, lived always in the country, and divided his time between his books and his hounds. His wife and daughter feldom mixed with people of their own rank, but **at** a horfe-race, or **a** rural vifit. And fee the effects! The girl, tho' fhe is naturally genteel, **has an** air of fimplicity.

BELMOUR.

But does not want fenfe.

MODELY.

No, no!—She has a devilifh deal of that kind of fenfe, which is acquired by early reading. I have heard her talk occafionally, like a queen in a tragedy, **or at leaft** like **a** fentimental lady **in a** comedy,

much

much above your miffes of thirty in town, I affure you.——As to the mother——But fhe is a character, and explains herfelf.

BELMOUR.

Yes, yes, I have read her. But pray how came it to pafs, that the father, who was of a different way of thinking in regard to party, fhould have left Sir John guardian to his daughter, with the additional claufe too, of her being obliged to marry him.

MODELY.

Why that is fomewhat furprizing. But the truth of the cafe was, they were thoroughly acquainted, and each confidered party as the foible of the other. Sir Harry thought a good hufband his daughter's beft fecurity for happinefs, and he knew it was impoffible Sir John Dorilant fhould prove a bad one.

BELMOUR.

And yet this profpect of happinefs would you deftroy.

MODELY.

No, no; I only fee farther than Sir Harry did, and would increafe that happinefs, by giving her a better hufband.

BELMOUR.

O! your humble fervant, Sir.

MODELY.

Befides, the mother is entirely in my intereft, and by the by has a hankering after Sir John herfelf. " He is a fober man, and fhould have a woman of " difcretion for his wife, not a hoydening girl."— 'Egad, Belmour, fuppofe you attacked the widow ? The woman is young enough, and has an excellent jointure.

BEL.

BELMOUR.

And so became your father-in-law.

MODELY.

You will have an admirable opportunity to-night; we are to have the fiddles you know, and you may dance with her.

When musick softens, and when dancing fires! Eh! Belmour!

BELMOUR.

You are vastly kind to Sir John, and would ease him I find of both his mistresses. But suppose this man of honour should be fool enough to resign his mistress, may not another kind of honour oblige him to run you through the body for deserting his sister?

MODELY.

Why faith, it may. However, it is not the first duel I have fought on such an occasion, so I am his man. Not that it is impossible but he may have scruples there too.

BELMOUR.

You don't think him a coward?

MODELY.

I know he is not. But your reasoning men have strange distinctions. They are quite different creatures, as I told you, from you and I.

BELMOUR.

You are pleased to compliment. But suppose now, as irrational as you think me, I should find out a means to make this whole affair easy to you?

MODELY.

How do you mean?

BELMOUR.

Not by attacking the widow, but by making my addresses in good earnest to Araminta.

C   MODE-

MODELY.

I forbid that abſolutely.

BELMOUR.

What, do you think it poſſible I ſhould ſucceed after the accompliſhed Mr. Modely?

MODELY.

Why faith between you and I, I think not, but I don't chuſe to hazard it.

BELMOUR.

Then you love her ſtill?

MODELY.

I confeſs it.

BELMOUR.

And it is nothing upon earth but that inſatiable vanity of yours, with a little tincture of avarice, that leads you a gadding thus?

MODELY.

I plead guilty. But be it as it will, I am determined to purſue my point. And ſee where the little rogue comes moſt opportunely. I told you ſhe would be here. Go, go, Belmour, you muſt not liſten to all my love ſcenes.   [*Exit Belmour.*
Now for a ſerious face, a little upon the tragic; young girls are mighty fond of deſpairing lovers.

Enter **C Æ L I A.**

C Æ L I A (**with** an affected ſurprize.)
Mr. Modely!——are you here?——I am come to meet my mama—I did not think to find you here.

MODELY.

Are you ſorry to find me here, madam?

CÆLIA.

Why ſhould I be ſorry, Mr. Modely?

MODELY.

May I hope you are pleased with it?

CÆLIA.

I have no dislike to company.

MODELY.

But is all company alike? Surely one would chuse one's companions. Would it have been the same thing to you, if you had met Sir John Dorilant here?

CÆLIA.

I should be very ungrateful if I did not like Sir John Dorilant's company. I am sure I have all the obligations in the world to him, and so had my poor papa. *(sighing.*

MODELY.

Whatever were your papa's obligations, his gratitude I am sure was unbounded. —— O that I had been his friend!

CÆLIA.

Why should you wish that, Mr. Modely? —— You would have had a great loss in him.

MODELY.

I believe I should. But I might likewise have had a confolation for that loss, which would have contained in it all earthly happiness.

CÆLIA.

I don't understand you.

MODELY.

He might have left his Cælia to me.

CÆLIA.

Dear, how you talk!

MODELY.

Talk, madam! —— O I could talk for ever, would you but listen to my heart's soft language, nor cruelly affect to disbelieve when I declare I love you.

CÆLIA.

Love *me*, Mr. Modely?———Are not you in love with Araminta?

MODELY.

I once thought I was.

CÆLIA.

And do lovers ever change?

MODELY.

No: thofe who feel a real paffion. But there are falfe alarms in love, which the unpractifed heart fometimes miftakes for true ones.

CÆLIA.

And were yours fuch for Araminta?

MODELY.

Alas, I feel they were. *(Looking earneftly at her.)*

CÆLIA.

You don't intend to marry her then, I hope.

MODELY.

Do you hope I fhould not marry her?

CÆLIA.

To be fure I do. I would not have the poor lady deceived, and I would willingly have a better opinion of Mr. Modely than to believe him capable of making falfe proteftations.

MODELY.

To you he never could.

CÆLIA.

To me?——I am out of the queftion.——But I am forry for Araminta, for I believe fhe loves you.

MODELY.

If you can pity thofe who love in vain, why am not I an object of compaffion?

CÆLIA.

Dear Mr. Modely, why will you talk thus? My hand, you know, is deftined to Sir John Dorilant,

rilant, and my duty there does not even permit me to think of other lovers.

MODELY.

Happy, happy man! Yet give me leave to afk one queftion, madam.——I dread to do it, tho' my laft glimpfe of happinefs depends upon your anfwer.

CÆLIA.

What queftion?——Nay, pray fpeak, I intreat it of you.

MODELY.

Then tell me, lovely Cælia, fincerely tell me, were your choice left free, and did it depend upon you only to determine who fhould be the mafter of your affections, might I expect one favourable thought?

CÆLIA (after fome hefitation.)

It—it does not depend upon me.

MODELY.

I know it does not, but if it did?

CÆLIA.

Come, come, Mr. Modely, I cannot talk upon this fubject. Impoffibilities are impoffibilities.—— But I hope you will acquaint Araminta inftantly with this change in your inclinations.

MODELY.

I would do it, but I dare not.

CÆLIA.

You fhould break it firft to Sir John.

MODELY.

My difficulty does not lie in the breaking it; but if I confefs my paffion at an end, I muft no longer expect admittance into this family, and I could ftill wifh to talk to Cælia as a friend.

CÆLIA.

Indeed, Mr. Modely, I fhould be loth myfelf to lofe your acquaintance; but —— O here comes my mama, fhe may put you in a method.

Enter

Enter LADY BEVERLEY.

LADY.

In any method, my dear, which decency and reserve will permit. Your servant, cousin Modely. What, you are talking strangely to this girl now?— O you men!

MODELY.

Your ladyship knows the sincerity of my passion here.

CÆLIA (with surprize.)

Knows your sincerity?

LADY.

Well, well, what signifies what I know?— You was mentioning some method I was to put you in.

CÆLIA.

Mr. Modely, madam, has been confessing to me that he no longer loves Araminta.

LADY.

Hum!—why such things may happen, child. We are not all able to govern our affections. But I hope if he breaks off with her, he will do it with decency.

MODELY.

That, madam, is the difficulty.

LADY.

What!——Is it a difficulty to be decent? Fie, fie, Mr. Modely.

MODELY.

Far be it from me even to think so, madam, before a person of your ladyship's reserved behaviour. But considering how far I have gone in the affair——

LADY.

Well, well, if that be all, I may perhaps help you out, and break it to Sir John myself.—— Not that I approve of roving affections I assure you.

MODE-

MODELY.

You bind me ever to you. —— But there is another cause which you alone can promote, and on which my eternal happiness ——

LADY.

Leave us—leave us, cousin Modely. I must not hear you talk in this extravagant manner.——
[*Pushing him towards the scene, and then aside to him.*]
—— I shall bring it about better in your absence. Go, go, man, go. [*Exit Modely.*
A pretty kind of a fellow really.——Now Cælia, come nearer, child: I have something of importance to say to you.——What do you think of that gentleman?

CÆLIA.

Of Mr. Modely, madam?

LADY.

Ay Mr. Modely, my cousin Modely.

CÆLIA.

Think of him, madam?

LADY.

Ay, think of him, child; you are old enough to think sure after the education I have given you. Well, what answer do you make?

CÆLIA.

I really don't understand your Ladyship's question.

LADY.

Not understand me, child? Why I ask you how you like Mr. Modely? What should you think of him as a husband.

CÆLIA.

Mr. Modely as a husband! Why surely madam, Sir John ——

LADY.

LADY.

Fiddle faddle Sir John ; Sir John knows better things than to plague himself with a wife in leading strings.

CÆLIA.

Is your ladyship sure of that ?

LADY.

O ho! would you be glad to have me sure of it ?

CÆLIA.

I don't know what I should be glad of. I would not give Sir John a moment's pain to be mistress of the whole world.

LADY.

But if it should be brought about without giving him pain. Hey ! Cælia——[*Patting her cheek with her fan.*

CÆLIA.

I should be sorry for it.

LADY.

Hey day !

CÆLIA.

For then he must think lightly of me.

LADY.

What does the girl mean ? Come, come, I must enter roundly into this affair. Here, here, sit down, and tell me plainly and honestly without equivocation or reservation, is Modely indifferent to you ? Nay, nay,——look me in the face; turn your eyes towards me. One judges greatly by the eyes, especially in a woman. Your poor papa used to say that my eyes reasoned better than my tongue. —— Well, and now tell me without blushing, is Modely indifferent to you ?

CÆLIA.

CÆLIA.

I fear he is not, madam, and it is that which perplexes me.

LADY.

How do you feel when you meet him?

CÆLIA.

Fluttered.

LADY.

Hum! —— While you are with him?

CÆLIA.

Fluttered.

LADY.

Hum! —— When you leave him?

CÆLIA.

Fluttered still.

LADY.

Strong symptoms truly!

CÆLIA.

When Sir John Dorilant talks to me, my heart is softened but not perplexed. My esteem, my gratitude overflows towards him. I consider him as a kinder father, with all the tenderness without the authority.

LADY.

But when Mr. Modely talks?

CÆLIA.

My tranquility of mind is gone, I am pleased with hearing what I doubt is flattery, and when he grasps my hand ——

LADY.

Well, well, I know all that. —— Be decent, child. —— You need say no more, Mr. Modely is the man. [*Rising.*

D CÆLIA.

CÆLIA.

But, dear Madam, there are a thousand obstacles.
—I am afraid Sir John loves me; I am sure he
esteems me, and I would not forfeit his esteem for
the universe. I am certain I can make him an affectionate and an humble wife, and I think I can
forget Mr. Modely.

LADY.

Forget a fiddle! Don't talk to me of forgetting.
I order you on your **duty** not to forget. Mr.
Modely is, and shall be the man. You may trust
my prudence **for** bringing it about. I will talk
with Sir John instantly.——I know what you are
going to say, but I will not hear a word of it. Can
you imagine, Cælia, that I shall do any thing but
with the utmost decency and decorum?

CÆLIA.

I know you will not, madam; but there are delicacies——

LADY.

With which I am unacquainted to be sure, and
my daughter must instruct me in them. Pray,
Cælia, where did you learn this nicety of sentiments?
Who was it that inspired them?

CÆLIA.

But the maxims of the world ——

LADY.

Are altered, I suppose, since I was of your age.
Poor thing, what world hast thou seen? Notwithstanding your delicacies and your maxims, Sir John
perhaps may be wiser than you imagine, and chuse a
wife of somewhat more experience.

CÆLIA.

May he be happy wherever he chuses.——But
dear madam ——

LADY.

LADY.

Again? don't make me angry. I will pofitively not be inftructed. Ay, you may well blufh. —— Nay, no tears —— Come, come, Cælia, I forgive you. I had idle delicacies myfelf once. Lard! I remember when your poor papa —— he, he, he —— but we have no time for old ftories. **What** would you fay now if Sir John himfelf fhould propofe it, and perfuade the match, **and** yet continue **as** much your friend as ever, nay become more fo, a nearer friend.

CÆLIA.

In fuch a cafe, madam ——

LADY.

I underftand you, and will about it inftantly? B'ye Cælia; O how its little heart flutters!

[*Exit Lady.*

CÆLIA.

It does indeed. A **nearer** friend? **I** hardly know whether I fhould wifh her fuccefs or not — Sir John is fo affectionate. Would **I** had never feen Mr. Modely! —— Araminta too! what will fhe fay? —— O I fee a thoufand bad confequences. I muft follow her, and prevent them.

END of the FIRST ACT.

ACT II.

SCENE *continues.*

LADY BEVERLEY *and* MODELY.

LADY.

PRITHEE don't teize me fo; I vow, coufin Modely, you are almoft as peremptory as my daughter. She truly was teaching me decorum juft now, and plaguing me with her delicacies, and her ftuff. I tell you Sir John will be in the garden immediately, this is always his hour of walking : and when he comes, I fhall lay the whole affair before him, with all its concatenation of circumftances, and I warrant you bring it about.

MODELY.

I have no doubt, madam, of the tranfcendency of your ladyfhip's rhetorick ; it is on that I entirely rely. But I muft beg leave to hint, that Araminta already fufpects my paffion, and fhould it be openly declared, would undoubtedly prevail that inftant with her brother to forbid me the houfe.

LADY.

Why, that might be.

MODELY.

And tho' I told your daughter I did not care how foon it came to an eclaircifment, yet a woman of your ladyfhip's penetration and knowledge of
the

the world, muſt ſee the neceſſity of concealing it,
at leaſt for a time. I beg pardon for offering what
may have even the diſtant appearance of inſtruction.
But it is Sir John's delicacy which muſt be princi-
pally alarmed with apprehenſions of her diſregard
for him; and I am ſure your ladyſhip's manner of
doing it, will ſhew him where he might much
better place his affections, and with an undoubted
proſpect of happineſs.

LADY.

Ay, now you talk to the purpoſe.--But ſtay, is not
that Sir John coming this way?—It is I vow, and
Araminta with him. We'll turn down this walk,
and reaſon the affair a little more, and then I will
come round the garden upon him.

[Modely takes her hand to lead her out.
You are very gallant, couſin Modely. *[Exeunt.*

Enter SIR JOHN DORILANT *and* ARAMINTA.

ARAMINTA.

What do you drag me into the garden for? We
were private enough where we were —— and I hate
walking.

SIR JOHN.

Forgive me, my dear ſiſter; I am reſtleſs every
where, my head and heart are full of nothing but
this lovely girl.

ARAMINTA.

My dear, dear brother, you are enough to ſpoil
any woman in the univerſe. I tell you again and
again, the girl is a good girl, an excellent girl, and
will make an admirable wife. You may truſt one
woman in her commendations of another; we are
not

I

not apt to be too favourable in our judgments, especially when there is beauty in the case.

SIR JOHN.

You charm me when you talk thus. If she is really all this, how happy must the man be who can engage her affections. But alas! Araminta, in every thing which regards me, it is duty, not love, which actuates her behaviour. She steals away my very soul by her attentions, but never once expresses that heart-felt tenderness, those sympathetic feelings.

ARAMINTA.

Ha—ha—ha!——O my stars!——Sympathetic feelings!——Why, would you have a girl of her age have those sympathetic feelings, as you call them! If she had, take my word for it, she would coquet it with half the fellows in town before she had been married a twelvemonth. Besides, Sir John, you don't consider that you was her father's friend; she has been accustomed from her infancy to respect you in that light; and our fathers friends, you know, are always old people, grey beards, philosophers, enemies to youth, and the destruction of gayety.

SIR JOHN.

But I was never such.

ARAMINTA.

You may imagine so; but you always had a grave turn. I hated you once myself.

SIR JOHN.

Dear Araminta!

ARAMINTA.

I did as I hope to live; for many a time has your aversion to dancing hindered me from having a fiddle.--By the by, remember we are to have the fiddles

to night.—But let that pass. As the case now stands,
if I was not already so near akin to you, you have
the temper in the world which I should chuse in a
husband.

SIR JOHN

That is obliging, however.

ARAMINTA.

Not so very obliging perhaps neither. It would
be merely for my own sake, for then would I have the
appearance of the most obedient sympathetic wife
in the universe, and yet be as despotic in my govern-
ment as an eastern monarch. And when I grew tired,
as I probably should do, of a want of contradiction,
why, I should find an easy remedy for that too——
I could break your heart in about a month.

SIR JOHN.

Don't trifle with me, 'tis your serious advice
I want; give it me honestly as a friend, and tenderly as a sister.

ARAMINTA.

Why I have done it, fifty times. What can I say
more? If you will have it again you must. This
then it is in plain terms.—But you are sure you are
heartily in love with her?

SIR JOHN.

Pshaw!

ARAMINTA.

Well then, that we will take for granted; and
now you want to know what is right and proper for
you to do in the case. Why, was I in your place,
I should make but short work with it. She knows
the circumstances of her father's will, therefore,
would I go immediately to her, tell her how my
heart stood inclined, and hope she had no objections
to comply, with what it is not in her power to
refuse.

SIR

SIR JOHN.

You would not have me talk thus abruptly to her?

ARAMINTA.

Indeed I would. It will fave a world of trouble. She will blufh perhaps at firft, and look a little aukward, (and by the by fo will you too); but if fhe is the girl I take her for, after a little irrefolute gefture, and about five minutes converfation, fhe will drop you a curtefy with the demure humility of a Veftal, and tell you it fhall be as you and her mama pleafes.

SIR JOHN.

O that it were come to that!

ARAMINTA.

And pray what hinders it? Nothing upon earth but your confummate prudence and difcretion.

SIR JOHN.

I cannot think of marrying her, till I am fure fhe loves me.

ARAMINTA.

Lud, Lud!—why what does that fignify? If fhe confents is not that enough?

SIR JOHN.

Her gratitude may induce her to confent, rather than make me unhappy.

ARAMINTA.

You would abfolutely make a woman mad.

SIR JOHN.

Why, could you think of marrying a man who had no regard for you.

ARAMINTA.

The cafe is widely different, my good cafuiftical brother; and perhaps I could not —— unlefs I was very much in love with him.

SIR

SIR JOHN.

And could you then?

ARAMINTA.

Yes I could —————— to tell you the truth I believe
I shall.

SIR JOHN.

What do you mean?

ARAMINTA.

I shall not tell you.——You have business enough
of your own upon your hands.

SIR JOHN.

Have you any doubts of Modely?

ARAMINTA.

I shall keep **them** to myself if I have.   For you
are a wretched counsellor in a **love** case.

SIR JOHN.

But dear Araminta——

ARAMINTA.

But dear **Sir** John Dorilant, you may make yourself perfectly easy, for you shall positively know nothing of my affairs.   As to your own, if you do not
instantly resolve to speak to Cælia, I will go and
talk **to her** myself.

SIR JOHN.

Stay, lady Beverley is coming towards us.

ARAMINTA.

And has left my swain yonder by himself.

SIR JOHN.

Suppose I break it to her?

ARAMINTA.

It is not a method which I should advise; but do
as you please. —— I know that horrid woman's sentiments very exactly, and I shall be glad to have
her teized a little (*Aside.*) —— I'll give you an op-

E   portunity

portunity by leaving you; and so adieu, my dear
sentimental brother!

We'll change partners if you please, madam — [*To
lady Beverley as she enters. —— And then exit to
[Modely.*

LADY BEVERLEY.

Poor mistaken creature! how fond the thing is!--
[*Aside, and looking after Araminta.*
Your servant, Sir John.

SIR JOHN.

Your ladyship's most obedient. —— [*After some
irresolute gesture on both sides —— lady Beverley
speaks.*]

LADY.

I-- I--- have wanted an opportunity of speaking
to you, Sir John, a great while.

SIR JOHN.

And I, madam, have long had an affair of consequence to propose to your ladyship.

LADY.

An affair of consequence to me! —— O Lud——
you will please to speak, Sir.

SIR JOHN

Not till I have heard your ladyship's commands.

LADY.

What, must women speak first? Fie, Sir John ——
(*looking languishingly*) —— Well then, the matter in
short is this, I have been long thinking how to dis-
pose of my girl properly. She is grown a woman
you see, and tho' I who am her mother say it, has
her allurements.

SIR JOHN.

Uncommon ones indeed.

LADY.

LADY.

Now I would willingly confult with **you** how to get her well married, before fhe is tainted with the indecorums of the world.

SIR JOHN.

It was the very fubject which I propofed fpeaking to you upon.—— I am forry to put your ladyfhip in mind of a near and dear lofs—But **you** remember Sir Harry's will.

LADY.

Yes, **yes,** I remember it very well. **Poor man !** it was undoubtedly the only weak thing **he was** ever guilty of.

SIR JOHN.

Madam !

LADY.

I fay, Sir, John we muft pardon the failings of our deceafed friends. Indeed his affection for his child excufes **it.**

SIR JOHN.

Excufes **it !**

LADY.

Yes indeed does it. His fondnefs for her might naturally make him wifh to place her with a perfon of **your** known excellence of character ; for my **own** part, had I died, I fhould **have wifhed it** myfelf.—**I don't** believe you **have your equal in the** world.— **Nay,** dear Sir John, 'tis no compliment.—This I fay might make him not attend **to** the impropriety of the thing, and the reluctance a gentleman of your good fenfe and judgment muft undoubtedly have to accede to fo unfuitable **a** treaty. Efpecially as he could **not** but **know** there were women of difcretion in the world, who would be proud **of** an alliance where the profpect of felicity was fo inviting and unqueftionable.

SIR JOHN, (who had appeared uneasy all the time she was speaking.

What women, madam? I know of none.

LADY.

Sir John!—That is not quite so complaisant me-thinks —— to our sex, I mean.

SIR JOHN.

I beg your pardon, madam; I hardly know what I say. Your ladyship has disconcerted every thing I was going to propose to you.

LADY.

Bless me, Sir John!—I disconcerted every thing? How pray? I have been only talking to you in an open friendly manner, with regard to my daughter, our daughter indeed I might call her, for you have been a father to her. The girl herself always speaks of you as such.

SIR JOHN.

Speaks of me as a father?

LADY.

Why, more unlikely things have happened, Sir John.

SIR JOHN.

Than what, madam?

LADY.

Dear Sir John!—You put such peremptory ques-tions, you might easily understand what one meant methinks.

SIR JOHN.

I find, madam, I must speak plain at once.——Know then, my heart, my soul, my every thought of happiness is fixed upon that lovely girl.

LADY.

O astonishing! Well, miracles are not ceased, that's certain. But every body, they say, must do a foolish

thing

thing once in their lives.——And can you really
and ſeriouſly think of putting Sir Harry's will in
execution?

SIR JOHN.

Would I could!

LADY.

To be ſure the girl has a fine fortune.

SIR JOHN.

Fortune! I deſpiſe it. I would give it with all
my ſoul to any one who could engage me her affections.—Fortune! dirt.

LADY.

I am thunderſtruck!———

SIR JOHN. (Turning eagerly to her.)

O madam, tell me, ſincerely tell me, what method can I poſſibly purſue to make her think fa-
vourably of me! You know her inmoſt ſoul, you
know the tender moments of addreſs, the eaſy
avenues to her unpractiſed heart. Be kind, and
point them out. [Graſping her hand.

LADY.

I vow, Sir John, I don't know what to ſay to
you.—— Let go my hand.——You talked of
my diſconcerting you juſt now, I am ſure you diſ-
concert me with a witneſs.———(Aſide.) I did
not think the man had ſo much rapture in him.
He ſqueezed my hand with ſuch an emphaſis! I
may gain him perhaps at laſt.

SIR JOHN.

Why will you not ſpeak, madam? Can you ſee
me on the brink of deſperation, and not lend a friendly hand to my aſſiſtance?

LADY.

I have it——I have it——Alas, Sir John, what
ſignifies

fignifies what I can do! Can I anfwer for the inclinations of a giddy girl?

SIR JOHN

You know fhe is not fuch; her innocent mind
is yet untainted with the follies of her fex. And if
a life devoted to her fervice, without a wifh but
what regards her happinefs, can win her to be
mine ——

LADY.

Why that might go a great way with an unpre-
judiced mind. But when a firft paffion has taken
place.

SIR JOHN. (With amazement.)

What do you mean?

LADY.

To tell you the truth, I am afraid the girl is
not fo untainted as you imagine.

SIR JOHN.

You diftract me. —— How——when —— whom
can fhe have feen?

LADY.

Undoubtedly there is a man.

SIR JOHN.

Tell me who, that I may —— No, that I may
give her to him, and make her happy whatever becomes of me.

LADY.

That is generous indeed.—— So —— fo.   [*Afide.*

SIR JOHN.

But 'tis impoffible. I have obferved all her mo-
tions, all her attentions, with a lover's eye incapa-
ble of erring.——Yet ftay—has any body written to
her?

LADY.

There are no occafion for letters, when people
are in the fame houfe together.

2   SIR

SIR JOHN.

Confusion!

LADY.

I was going to offer some proposals to you, but your strange declaration stopped me short.

SIR JOHN.

You proposals? —— You?—— Are you her abetter in the affair? —— O madam, what unpardonable crime have I committed against you, that you should thus conspire my ruin? Have not I always behaved to you like a friend, a brother?—— I will not call you ungrateful.

LADY.

Mercy on us! ——The man raves.— How could it possibly enter into my head, or the girl's either, that you had any serious thoughts of marrying her? But I see you are too much discomposed at present, to admit of calm reasoning. So I shall take some other opportunity.——Friend——Brother——Ungrateful!—Marry come up!— I hope, at least, you will not think of forcing the poor girl's inclinations! Ungrateful indeed! [Exit in a passion.

SIR JOHN.

Not for the universe.——Stay, madam.——She is gone.—— But it is no matter. I am but little disposed for altercation now. Heigh ho! — Good heaven! can so slight an intercourse have effected all this? — I have scarce ever seen them together. O that I had been born with Belmour's happy talents of address.—— Address!——'tis absolute magick,'tis fascination — Alas! 'tis the rapidity of real passion. —— Why did Modely bring him hither to his wedding? Every thing has conspired against me. He brought him, and the delay of the lawyers has kept him here. Had I taken Araminta's advice a poor fortnight ago, it had not been in the power of fate to have undone me. — And yet she might
have

have seen him afterwards, which would at least have made her duty uneasy to her. —— Heigh ho!

Enter ARAMINTA *and* MODELY.

ARAMINTA. (Entering.)

I tell you, I heard them very loud! and I will see what is the matter.   O! here is my brother alone.

SIR JOHN. (Taking her tenderly by the hand.)

O Araminta ! —— I am loft beyond redemption.

ARAMINTA.

Dear brother, what can have happened to you ?

SIR JOHN. (Turning to Modely.)

Mr. Modely, you could not intend it, but you have ruined me.

MODELY. (Alarmed.)

I, Sir John !

SIR JOHN.

You have brought a friend with you, who has pierced me to the very foul.

MODELY.

Belmour !

SIR JOHN.

He has stolen my Cælia's affections from me.

ARAMINTA. (Looking flyly at Modely.)

Belmour !

MODELY.

This must be a mistake, but I'll humour it. (*Aside.*)   It cannot be, who can have told you so ?

SIR JOHN.

Her mother has been this instant with me, to make proposals on the subject.

MODELY.

For Belmour !

SIR JOHN.

She did not absolutely mention his name, but I

could

could not miſtake it. For ſhe told me the favoured
lover was under the ſame roof with us.

MODELY. (*A little diſconcerted.*)

I could not have believed it of him.

ARAMINTA.

Nor do I yet.— [*Looking ſlyly again at Modely.*

MODELY.

There muſt certainly be ſome miſtake in it; at
the worſt, I am ſure I can prevail ſo far with Belmour, as to make him drop his pretenſions.

SIR JOHN.

You cannot make her ceaſe to love him. [*Sighing.*

MODELY.

Time may eaſily get the better of ſo young a
paſſion.

SIR JOHN.

Never, never; ſhe is too ſincere, too delicately
ſenſible.

MODELY.

Come, come, you muſt not think ſo; it is not yet
gone ſo far, but that it may be totally forgotten.—
Now for a maſter-ſtroke to clench the whole——
(*Aſide.*) In the mean time, Sir John, I have the
ſatisfaction of acquainting you, that my affair, with
Araminta's leave, draws very near a concluſion.
The lawyers have finiſhed their papers, and I only
now wait for your peruſal of them.

ARAMINTA. (*Aſide.*)

Well ſaid!

MODELY.

I ordered the writings to be laid upon your table.

ARAMINTA. (*Aſide.*)

What does he mean?

SIR JOHN.

Dear Mr. Modely, you ſhall not wait a moment
for me. I will diſpatch them inſtantly. I feel the

want of happiness too severely myself, to postpone it
in others. I leave you with my sister; when she
names the day, you may depend upon my concurrence. [*Exit Sir John.*

(MODELY and ARAMINTA look at one another for some time, then he speaks.)

I hope, madam, you are now convinced of my
sincerity.

ARAMINTA.

I am absolutely struck dumb with your assurance.

MODELY. (With an affected surprize.)
Madam!

ARAMINTA.

You cannot mean all this.

MODELY.

Why not, madam?

ARAMINTA.

Why, don't you know that I know————

MODELY.

I cannot help a lady's knowledge or imagina-
tions. All I know is, that it is in your power to
make me either the happiest or most miserable man
in the whole creation.

ARAMINTA.

Well, this is astonishing.

MODELY.

I am sorry, madam, that any unguarded behaviour of mine, any little playful gallantries, should
have occasioned surmises, which————

ARAMINTA.

Serious, as I hope to live.

MODELY.

Is it not enough to make one serious, when the
woman one has pursued for years, almost with adoration, is induced by mere appearances to doubt
the

the honourableneſs of one's intentions. Have you
not heard me this moment apply to your brother,
even in the midſt of his uneaſineſs.——I little expected where the difficulty would lie.

ARAMINTA.

Well, well, poor thing, I won't teize it any longer; here, there, take my hand.

MODELY.

Duped by Jupiter.—— (*Aſide.*)——O my ever-
laſting treaſure! And when, and when ſhall I be
happy?

ARAMINTA.

It ſhall depend upon yourſelf.

MODELY.

To-morrow, then, my angel, be the day. O
Araminta, I cannot ſpeak my tranſport.——And
did you really think that I was in love with Cælia?

ARAMINTA.

Why, as a proof of my future ſincerity, I muſt
confeſs I did.

MODELY.

I wonder how you could.

ARAMINTA.

Come, come, there were grounds enough for a
woman in love to go upon.

MODELY. (taking her by the hand.)
But you are now perfectly eaſy?

ARAMINTA. (pulling her hand from him.)
Why, yes, I think I am.——But what can
my brother mean about Belmour?

MODELY.

It is ſome trick of the widow's.

ARAMINTA.

I dare ſay ſhe meant you.

MODE-

MODELY.

Poffibly fhe might ; you know her motives.

ARAMINTA.

Yes, yes, her paffion for my brother is pretty notorious. But the wretch will be miftaken.——To-morrow, you fay ?

MODELY.

To-morrow, my adorable.

ARAMINTA.

It fhall be as you pleafe.——But my fituation is fo terribly aukward, that I muft break from you. Adieu !   [*Exit Araminta.*

MODELY.

Upon my foul fhe is a fine woman ; and loves me to diftraction; and what is ftill more, I moft undoubtedly love her.——I have a good mind to take her.——Yet not to have it in my power to fucceed in the other place, would call my parts in queftion.——No, no;—I muft not difparage my parts neither.——In order to be a great character, one fhould go as near being a rogue as poffible. I have a philofopher's opinion on my fide in that, and the practice of half the heroes and politicians in Europe.

END of the SECOND ACT.

ACT III.

SCENE continues.

BELMOUR (alone.)

CÆLIA in love with me! Egad the thing is not impoſſible; my friend Modely may have been a little miſtaken. Sir John was very ſerious when he told me of it; and though I proteſted to him that I had never made the leaſt advances, he ſtill perſiſted in his opinion.—The girl muſt have have told him ſo herſelf.—Let me recollect a little. —— She is always extremely civil to me; but that indeed ſhe is to every body.—I do not remember any thing particular in her looks; but I ſhall watch them more narrowly the next time I ſee her.—She is very handſome; and yet in my opinion, notwithſtanding Modely's infidelity, Araminta is much the finer woman.—Suppoſe—— No, that will not do.

Enter MODELY.

MODELY.

So, ſo, Mr. Belmour, I imagined I ſhould find you here; this is the lover's corner. We have all had our reveries in it. But why don't you talk louder, man? You ought, at leaſt, to give me my revenge in that. My ſoliloquies, you know, are eaſily over-heard.

BEL-

BELMOUR.

I never defignedly over-heard them, Mr. Modely; nor did I make any improper ufe of the accident.

MODELY.

Grave, very grave, and perfectly moral! And fo this is all I am to have for the lofs of my miftrefs.——— Heigh ho!

Then I muft be content to fee her blefs
Yon happier youth.———

BELMOUR.

Your raillery is a little unfeafonable, Mr. Modely; for to fpeak plainly, I begin to fufpect that this is fome trick of yours, to dupe me as well as Sir John Dorilant.

MODELY.

Upon my honour, no, if we muft be ferious: it may be a miftake, but not intended on my fide, I can affure you. Come, come, if the girl really likes you, take her. If I fhould prove the happy man, give me joy, and there's an end of it.

BELMOUR.

I fancy you are ufed to difappointments in love, they fit fo eafy upon you. Or rather I fhould fuppofe, in this cafe, you are pretty fure of your ground.

MODELY.

Neither, upon my foul; but a certain *Je ne fcai quoy*, a *Gayete de Coeur* which carries me above misfortunes: fome people call it vanity.

BELMOUR.

And are not abfolutely miftaken. But what becomes of Araminta all this while?

MODELY. (yawning.)

I fhall marry her, I believe, to-morrow.

BEL.

4

BELMOUR.

Marry her?

MODELY.

Yes, Sir John is at this very moment looking over the settlements.

BELMOUR.

I don't understand you.

MODELY.

And yet it is pretty plain, methinks. I tell you I am to be married to-morrow. Was it not time to make sure of one mistress, when you was running away with the other?

BELMOUR.

You know I have no such intentions.———— But are you really serious? Have you laid aside your designs upon Cælia?

MODELY.

Not so, neither.

BELMOUR.

What do you mean then by your marriage with Araminta? Why won't you unriddle this affair to me?

MODELY.

Because it is at present a riddle to myself, and I expect lady Beverley here every moment to resolve the enigma.

BELMOUR.

Was it a scheme of her's?

MODLEY.

Certainly, and I partly guess it, but will not unbosom till I know it fully.—— Come, come, with all that gravity of countenance and curiosity, you must leave me instantly; the lady will be here, and the plot unravelled, and then ————

BEL-

BELMOUR.

I shall expect to be satisfied. [*Exit.*

MODELY.

Ha! ha! ha! or elfe you fight me, I suppose. Why, so you may; and so may Sir John Dorilant too, and faith with some colour of reason. But my comfort is, that I have experience on my side, and if I survive the rencounter, I shall be a greater hero than ever amongst the ladies, and be esteemed in all companies as much a man of honour as the best of you.

Enter LADY BEVERLEY.

LADY.

Dear cousin Modely, I am all over in an agitation; we shall certainly be discovered; that devil Araminta ———

MODELY.

What of her, madam?

LADY.

Is now with her brother talking so eagerly ——— Oh! I saw the villainous changes in her countenance; I would have given the world to have overheard their conversation.—Come, come, you must advise me instantly.

MODELY.

Your ladyship must first let me into the secret. I am absolutely in a wood with regard to the whole affair. What is all this of Cælia and Belmour?

LADY.

Nothing, nothing at all; an errant dilemma of the foolish man's own making, which his impertinent sister will immediately clear up to him, and when all must out.

MODE-

MODELY.

But how came Belmour ever to be mentioned in the cafe?

LADY.

Dear, dear, he never was mentioned. I muft confefs that I was fo provoked with Sir John's un-natural behaviour, that I could not help telling him that Cælia had a lover, and in the houfe too. Your fituation with regard to Araminta made him never dream of you, and confequently all his fufpicions turned on Belmour.

MODELY.

But you did not fay that that lover had made his addreffes to Cælia?

LADY.

I don't know what I might fay; for he ufed me like a Turk. But whatever I faid I can unfay it again.

MODELY.

Why, if I might venture to advice a perfon of your lady's fagacity!——

LADY.

O ay, with all my heart, coufin Modely. For though I may fay it without vanity, that nobody has a more clear apprehenfion of things when the mental faculty is totally undifturbed; yet, when I am in a trepidation, nobody upon earth can be more glad of advice.

MODELY.

Why, then, madam, to fpeak with reverence, I fhould hope your ladyfhip would fee the neceffity of keeping me as concealed as poffible. It is the young lady's paffion, not mine, which muft have the principal influence. Sir John Dorilant's pecu-liarity of temper is fuch——

G LADY.

L A D Y.

Yes, yes, he has peculiarity enough, that's certain.

M O D E L Y.

And it is there, madam, as the weakeft part, that our attack will be the fureft. If fhe confeffes an inclination for me, not both the Indies, added to her fortune, could induce him to marry her.

L A D Y.

That is honourable, however, coufin Modely. But he is a horrid creature, notwithftanding.

M O D E L Y.

I grant it, madam; but a failure in an improper purfuit may recal his reafon, and, as he does not want underftanding, teach him to fearch for happinefs where only it is to be expected.

L A D Y.

He! he! I am fo angry with him at prefent, that I really believe I fhould refufe him.

M O D E L Y.

Your ladyfhip muft not be too cruel.

L A D Y.

Why, I confefs it is not in my nature; but—blefs me, here they come. ———— Let us run down this walk directly, for they muft not fee us together. [*Exeunt.*

Enter A R A M I N T A *and* S I R J O H N D O R I L A N T.

A R A M I N T A.

Come along, I fay, you dragged me into the garden juft now, and I will command in my turn. Talk to her, you muft and fhall. The girl has fenfe and fpirit when fhe is difengaged from that
horrid

horrid mother of her's ; and I have told her you
wanted her, and in this very fpot.

SIR JOHN.

You cannot feel, Araminta, what you make me
fuffer. But fooner or later it muft come to this,
and therefore I will affume a refolution, and be rid
of all my doubts at once.

ARAMINTA.

I tell you, this nonfenfe about Belmour is merely
a phantom of her mother's raifing, to found your
intentions, and promote her own.

SIR JOHN.

Thus far is certain, that Belmour difclaims all
knowledge of the affair, and with an appearance
of fincerity ; but even that is doubtful. Befides,
they are not his, but her inclinations which give me
any concern. It is the heart I require. The life-
lefs form, beauteous as it is, would only elude my
grafp; the fhadow of a joy, not the reality.

ARAMINTA.

Dear, dear, that men had but a little common
fenfe ; or that one could venture to tell them what
one knows of one's own fex! I have a good mind
to be honeft.——— As I live, the girl is coming.
——I'll fpeed her on the way. Courage, brother,
Voila !   [*Exit.*

SIR JOHN.

How fhall I begin with her ?——What ideots
are men when they have a real paffion ! ridiculous,
beneath contempt. ——— [*Walks about the ftage*]
———Suppofe ——— I will not fuppofe ; the honeft
heart fhall fpeak its faithful dictates, and if it fails,
——— why, let it.

Enter

Enter CÆLIA.

CÆLIA (with timidity.)

Araminta tells me, Sir, that you had something
to fay to me.

SIR JOHN.

I have, madam. ——Come forward, Mifs Beverley. —— Would you chufe to fit. ——— [*They fit
down.*] —— [*After fome irrefolute gefture.*] You are
not afraid of catching cold?

CÆLIA.

Not in the leaft, Sir.

SIR JOHN.

I know fitting in the open air has that effect
upon fome people —— but your conftitution is yet
untainted. —— Did my fifter fay any thing concerning the fubject I would fpeak to you upon?

CÆLIA.

She only told me, Sir, that it was of moment.

SIR JOHN.

It is of moment, indeed, Cælia. ——— But you
muft not think that I am angry.

CÆLIA.

Angry, Sir!

SIR JOHN.

I don't mean angry. —— I am a little confufed;
but I fhall recover myfelf prefently. ——[*Rifes, and
Cælia rifes too.*] —— Nay, pray fit, Mifs Beverley.
——— Whatever I feel myfelf, I would not difturb
you. ——[*Returns to his feat, then after a paufe,
goes on.*]——The affair I would fpeak to you upon
is this: —— You remember your father perfectly?

CÆLIA.

And ever fhall.

S I

SIR JOHN.

Indeed he was a good man, Miss Beverley, a virtuous man, and felt tenderly for your happiness. —— Those tears become you, and yet, methinks, I would not provoke them. ——When he died, he **left you** to my **care.**

CÆLIA.

Which alone made his loss supportable.

SIR JOHN.

Are you sincere in what you say?

CÆLIA.

I should be ungrateful indeed, if I was not.

SIR JOHN (turning towards her.)

Nay, you are sincerity itself. – O Cælia [*Taking her by the hand.*] ——But I beg your pardon, I am assuming a liberty I have no right to take, till you allow it.

CÆLIA.

Sir!

SIR JOHN.

I see I have alarmed you. —— Retire **Miss Be**verley. —— I'll speak to you some other time.—— [*She is going.*] —— Cælia, Miss Beverley, —— pray come back, my dear. —— I am afraid my behaviour is rather **too** abrupt. —— Perhaps, too, it may displease you.

CÆLIA.

I can be displeased with nothing from you, Sir; and am ready to obey you, be your commands what they will.

SIR JOHN.

Command, Cælia! ———— that's a hard word.

CÆLIA.

I am sorry it offends you.

SIR

3

SIR JOHN.

You know beft, Cælia, whether it ought to offend me; would I could read the fentiments of your
heart! Mine are but too apparent.——In fhort, my
dear, you know the purport of your father's will,
dare you fulfil it?

CÆLIA.

To the minuteft circumftance.—— It is my duty.

SIR JOHN.

Ah, Cælia, that word *duty* deftroys the obligation.

CÆLIA.

Sir!——

SIR JOHN.

I don't know how it is, but I am afraid to afk you
the only queftion, which fincerely anfwered, could
make me happy—or miferable.   [*Half afide.*

CÆLIA.

Let me beg of you, fir, to afk it freely.

SIR JOHN.

Well then —— is your heart your own?
O Cælia, that hefitation confirms my tears. You
cannot anfwer in the affirmative, and have too much
humanity for what I feel, to add to my torments.
—Good God! — and is it poffible, that an acquaintance of a few days, fhould entirely obliterate the at-
tentive affiduity, the tender anxieties which I have
fhewn for years!--But I underftand it all too well.
Mine were the aweful, though heart-felt attentions
of a parent; his, the fprightly addrefs of a prefum-
ing lover. His eafy affurance has won upon your
affections, and what I thought *my* greateft merit,
has undone me.

CÆLIA.

You were fo good, fir, a little while ago, to pity
my

my confusion; pity it now, and whilst I lay my heart open before you, be again that kind, that generous friend, which I have always found you.

SIR JOHN.

Go on.——

CÆLIA.

It is in vain for me to dissemble an ignorance of your meaning, nor would I if I could. I own I have been too much pleased with Mr. Modely's conversation.

SIR JOHN.

Modely's?

CÆLIA.

Let me go on.—— His intended marriage with Araminta, gave him a freedom in the family which it was not my business to restrain. His attentions to my mother, and the friendly manner in which he executed some commissions of consequence to her, gave him frequent opportunities of talking to me. I will confess too, that his appearance and his manner struck me. But I was so convinced of his real passion for Araminta, that I never dreamt of the least attachment to me, till——

SIR JOHN.

Till what, when— Modely ?——Why, he is to be married to my sister to-morrow or next day.

CÆLIA.

I know it was so intended, but his behaviour this morning, and the intercessions of my mother, had, I own, won upon me strongly, and induced me to believe that I only was the object of his pursuits.

SIR JOHN.

I am thunderstruck! ———

CÆLIA.

My mother made me clearly perceive that the
com-

completion of his marriage would be an injury to Araminta. She told me too, fir, that you yourfelf would be my advifer in the affair, and even perfuaded me to accept it.

SIR JOHN.

O the malicious woman!

CÆLIA.

In that indeed I perceive fhe greatly erred. And I only mean this as a confeffion of what is paft, and of what is now at an end for ever.——For the future, I give myfelf to your guidance alone, and am what you direct. ——— [*Giving her hand to him.*

SIR JOHN.

Thou amiable foftnefs!——— No, Cælia, however miferable I may be myfelf, I will not make you fo; it was your heart, not your hand I afpired to. As the former has been feduced from me, it would be an injuftice to us both to accept of the latter. As to Mr. Modely, and Lady Beverley, I have not deferved this treachery from them, and they fhall both feel my refentment.

CÆLIA.

Sir!

SIR JOHN.

She told me indeed there was a favoured lover, and my fufpicions fell very naturally upon Belmour. Nay, even now, nothing but that lovely fincerity— which undoes me—could make me credit this villainy of Modely. —— O Cælia! what a heart have I loft!

CÆLIA.

You cannot, fhall not lofe it; worthlefs as it is, 'tis yours, and only yours, my father, guardian, lover, hufband! [*Hangs upon him weeping.*

Enter

Enter **A R A M I N T A.**

A R A M I N T A.

Hey day! what a fcene is here! What is the matter with ye both.

S I R J O H N.

O fifter! that angel goodnefs, that mirror of her fex, has ruined me.

A R A M I N T A.

Ruined you! how?

S I R J O H N.

Nay, I am not the only fufferer, Modely is as falfe to you, as her mother is to all of us.

A R A M I N T A:

I don't underftand you.

S I R J O H N.

You will too foon. My fufpicions of Belmour were all a chimæra; it is your impious Modely who has poffeffion of her heart.——To me fhe is loft ir-recoverably.——   [*Going.*

A R A M I N T A.

Stay, brother.

S I R J O H N.

I cannot, my foul's too full.   [*Exit.*

A R A M I N T A:

Pray, mifs Beverley, what is the meaning of all this?

C Æ L I A.

I cannot fpeak——[*Throwing herfelf into a chair.*

A R A M I N T A.

I'll be hang'd if this fellow Modely has not talk-ed you into an opinion, that he is in love with you; indeed, my dear, your youth and inexperience may lead you into ftrange fcrapes; and that mother of

yours is enough to turn any girl's head in the uni-
verfe. Come, come, unriddle this affair to me.

CÆLIA.

Alas! madam, all I know is, that the only man
I ever did, or ever can efteem, defpifes me, and, I
fear, hates me.

ARAMINTA.

Hates you! he doats upon you to diftraction.——
But pray, did Modely ever make any ferious addreffes to you ?

CÆLIA.

Alas! but too often.

ARAMINTA.

The hypocrite! but I'll be even with him.——
And your mother, I fuppofe, encouraged him ? An
infamous woman ! But I know her drift well
enough.————

Enter **LADY BEVERLEY.**

LADY.

Where is my poor girl ? I met Sir John Dorilant in fuch a furious way, that he feems to have
loft all common civility. What have they done to
you, child ?

ARAMINTA.

Done to her ? What has your ladyfhip done
to her ? I knew **your little artifices** long ago,
but ——

LADY.

My artifices ! Mrs. Araminta.

ARAMINTA.

Your artifices, lady Beverley ; but they are all
to no purpofe; the girl has too good an underftanding to be impofed upon any longer; and your boaft-
ed

ed machinations are as vain and empty in their effect, as in their contrivance.

LADY.

What does the woman mean? But the loss of a
lover, I suppose, is an excuse for ill-breeding! Poor
creature! if the petulancy of thy temper would let
me, I could almost pity thee. The loss of a lover
is no agreeable thing; but women at our time of
life, Mrs. Araminta, must not expect a lasting passion.

ARAMINTA.

Scarce any at all I believe, if they go a wooing
themselves. For my part, I have had the satisfac-
tion of being sollicited however. And I am afraid
my rustic brother never gave your ladyship's sollicitations even the flightest encouragement. How
was it? Did you find him quite hard-hearted? No
bowels of compassion for so accomplished a
damsel?

CÆLIA. (interposing.)

Dear madam! dear Araminta!

LADY.

Stand away, child. —— Desert, madam, is not always attended with success, nor confidence neither.
There are some women so assured of their conquest,
as even to disgust a lover on the very day of
marriage.

ARAMINTA.

Was my behaviour ever such?

LADY.

I really cannot say, Mrs. Araminta; but the
world, you know, is censorious enough, when a
match is broken off so near its conclusion, as gene-
rally to charge the inconstancy of the lover on some
defect in his mistress.

H 2 ARA-

A R A M I N T A.

I defy him to produce any.

L A D Y.

And yet he has certainly left you ; " Never, ah " never to return."

A R A M I N T A.

Infolent!

C Æ L I A. (interpofing again.)

Dear Araminta!

A R A M I N T A.

But your ladyfhip may be miftaken even in that too.   I may find him at his follicitations again ; and if I do ————.

L A D Y.

You'll take him.

A R A M I N T A.

Take him ? ——Daggers and poifon fooner.

L A D Y.

Poor creature!—Come, Cælia, words do but aggravate her misfortune.   We only difturb her. You fee, my dear, what are the effects of too violent a paffion.   It may be a leffon for your future conduct.

A R A M I N T A.

Look you, lady Beverley, don't provoke me,

L A D Y.

Why, what will you do?

C Æ L I A. (interpofing.)

For heaven's fake, madam ————

L A D Y.

I fancy, Mrs. Araminta, inftead of quarrelling, we had better join forces.   If we could but get this girl out of the way, we might both fucceed.

A R A M I N T A.

You are a wicked woman. ——

LADY,

LADY.

Poor creature! shall I say any thing to my cousin Modely for you? You know I have weight with him.

ARAMINTA.

Yes, madam; you may tell him that his connections with you, have rendered him ridiculous; and that the revenge of an injured woman is never contemptible. [*Exit Araminta.*

LADY. (leading off Cælia on the other side.)

Poor creature!——Come along, child,

END of the THIRD ACT.

ACT IV.

SCENE *continues*.

SIR JOHN DORILANT, *alone*.

THIS fatal fpot, which draws me to it almoft involuntarily, muft be the fcene of another interview.——Thank heaven I have recovered myfelf. Nor fhall any mifery which I may fuffer, much lefs any profpect of a mean revenge, make me act unbecoming my character.

Enter ARAMINTA.

ARAMINTA.

Well, brother, I hope you are refolved to marry this girl.

SIR JOHN.

Marry her, my dear Araminta? Can you think it poffible, that I fhould have fo prepofterous a thought? No, my behaviour fhall deferve her, but not over-rule her inclinations. Were I to feize the tender opportunity of her prefent difpofition, the world would afcribe it to her fortune; and I am fure my deceafed and valuable friend, however kindly he meant to me in the affair, never intended that I fhould make his daughter unhappy.

ARA.

ARAMINTA.

But I tell you she loves you ; and you muft and fhall marry her.

SIR JOHN.

Ah fifter, you are willing to difpofe of her any way. That worthlefs lover of yours ftill hangs about your heart, and I have avoided feeing him on your account, as well as Cælia's.

ARAMINTA.

To fhew how miftaken you are in all this, I have given him up totally. I defpife, and hate him ; nay I am upon the brink of a refolution to give myfelf to another. [*Sir John fhakes his head.*
I am, I affure you ; his friend Mr. Belmour is by no means indifferent on my fubject.

SIR JOHN.

And is this revenge on yourfelf, a proof of your want of paffion for him ?—Ah Araminta!— Come, come, my dear, I own I think him unworthy of you, and would refent his ufage to the utmoft, did not I clearly perceive that it would appear mercenary in myfelf, and give real pain both to you and Cælia.

ARAMINTHA.

I actually don't know what to fay to you.

SIR JOHN.

You had better fay nothing. Your fpirits at prefent are too much alarmed. —I have fent for Cælia hither, a fhort hour may determine the fates of all of us. I know my honourable intentions will give her great uneafinefs. But it is my duty which exacts them from me.— You had better take a turn or two in fome other part of the garden ;— I fee my fteward coming this way :—I may want your affiftance but too foon. [*Exit Araminta.*
Enter

Enter STEWARD.

Have you brought thofe papers I bad you look out?

STEWARD.

Yes, Sir. But there is the gentleman within to wait upon your honour, concerning the eftate you intended to purchafe. It feems a mighty good bargain.

SIR JOHN.

I cannot fpeak to him now.

STEWARD.

Your honour always ufed to be punctual.

SIR JOHN.

Alas! Jonathan, I may be punctual again to-morrow.—Give me the papers. Did Mifs Beverley fay fhe would come to me?

STEWARD.

Immediately, Sir. But I wifh your honour would confider, fuch bargains as thefe do not offer every day.

SIR JOHN.

Heigh ho!

STEWARD.

It joins fo conveniently too to your honour's own eftate, within a hedge as I may fay.

SIR JOHN.

Prithee don't plague me.

STEWARD.

Nay, 'tis not my intereft, but your honour's. Tho' that indeed I may call my intereft, for I am fure I love your honour.

SIR JOHN.

I know thou doft, Jonathan, and I am too hafty,

I   but

—but leave me now.—If the gentleman will do me the favour of staying all night, I may satisfy him in the morning. My head and heart are too full now for any business which concerns my fortune.

STEWARD.

Something goes very wrong with my poor master. Some love nonsense or other I suppose——I wish all the women were in the bottom of the sea, for my part. [*Exit Steward.*

Enter **LADY BEVERLEY** *and*
CÆLIA.

LADY.

I thought it requisite, Sir John, as I heard you had something of importance to transact with my daughter, to wait upon you with her.

SIR JOHN.

Was that necessary, madam ?—I begged the favour of Miss Beverley's company only.

LADY.

But a mother, you know, Sir John, who has a tender concern for her child ——

SIR JOHN.

Should shew it upon every occasion.

LADY.

I find, Sir John, there is some misunderstanding at present, which a woman of prudence and experience might be much better consulted upon, than a poor young thing, whose —— -

SIR JOHN.

Not at all, madam ; Cælia has all the prudence I require, and our present conversation will soon be over.

I   LADY.

LADY.

Nay, Sir John, to be sure I am not afraid of trusting my daughter alone with you. A man of your discretion will undoubtedly be guilty of no impropriety. . But a third person sometimes, where the parties concerned are a little too much influenced by their passions, has occasioned very substantial, and very useful effects. I have known several instances of it, in the course of my experience.

SIR JOHN.

This, madam, will not be one of them.—How teizing!   *[Walking aside.*

LADY.

I find, Sir John, that you are determined to have your own way, and therefore I shall shew you by my behaviour, that I know what good manners require, tho' I do not always meet with the same treatment from other people.   *[Exit Lady.*

SIR JOHN.

Now, Cælia, we are alone, and I have many excuses to make to you for the impassioned sallies of our late conversation ; which I do most sincerely.—Can you pardon them ?

CÆLIA.

Alas! Sir, 'tis I who ought to intreat for pardon,

SIR JOHN.

Not in the least, madam, I have no blame to cast upon you for any part of your conduct. Your youth and inexperience, joined to the goodness of your heart, are sufficient apologies for any shadow of indiscretion which might appear in your behaviour. I am afraid mine was not so irreproachable. However, Cælia, I shall endeavour to make you all the amends in my power; and to shew you that it is your happiness, not my own, which is the object of my anxiety.

Your father's will is but too clear in its intentions. But the purity of his heart never meant to promote my felicity at the expence of yours. You are therefore, madam, entirely at liberty from this moment, to make your choice where you please. This paper will entitle you to that authority, and this will enable you to bestow your fortune where you bestow your hand.——Take them, my dear !——Why are you so disturbed ?——Alas, Cælia, I see too plainly the cause of these emotions. You only wish the happy man to whom you have given your heart, loved you as I do !——

But I beg pardon ; and will only add one caution, which my duty demands of me, as your guardian, your protector, and your father's friend. ——You have been a witness of Modely's transactions with my sister. Have a care therefore, Cælia ; be sure of his firm attachment before you let your own hurry you into a compliance. These papers give you up all power on my part ; but as an adviser, I shall be always ready to be consulted.

CÆLIA.

My tears and my confusion have hitherto hindered me from answering ; not the invidious suggestion which you have so cruelly charged me with. What friend, what lover have I, to engross my attentions ? I never had but one, and he has cast me off for ever.——O, Sir, give me the papers, and let me return them where my soul longs to place them.

SIR JOHN.

No, Cælia, to accept them again, would impeach the justice of my whole proceeding. It

would

would make it look like the mean artifice of a mercenary villain, who attempted to gain by stratagem what his merits did not entitle him to.——— I blush to think of it.—I have performed my office. Be mistress of yourself, and let me fly from a combat to which I find myself unequal. [*Exit Sir John.*

(CÆLIA sits down, leaning her head upon her hand.)

Enter MODELY *and* BELMOUR.
MODELY.

Hist! hist! he has just left her, and in a fine situation for my approaches.———— If you are not yet satisfied, I will make up all differences with you another time.——Get into the arbour, and be a witness of my triumph. You shall see me, like another Cæsar, Come, See—and Overcome.

[*Belmour goes into the arbour.*

(MODELY comes forward, walks two or three turns by her, bowing as he passes, without being taken notice of, then speaks.)

If it is not an interruption, madam, when I find you thus alone ——

CÆLIA (rising.)
I would chuse to be alone.

MODELY.
Madam!

CÆLIA (after a little pause.)
In short, Mr. Modely, your behaviour to me of late is what I can by no means approve of. It is unbecoming your character as a man of honour, and would be a stain to the ingenuous modesty of my sex for me to suffer it.

MODELY.
You surprize me, madam. Can the adoration of an humble love, the timid advances of a man whom

whom you beauty has undone, be such unpardonable offences?

(CÆLIA looks with indignation at him, and is going off.)

MODELY (catching hold of her, and falling upon his knees.)

Nay, madam, you must not leave me!

CÆLIA.

Rise, Sir, or I am gone this moment.———I thought of flying from you, but my foul disdains it.——— Know then, Sir, that I am mistress of myself, mistress of my fortune, and may bestow my hand wherever my heart directs it.

MODELY.

My angel!——   [Coming eagerly up to her.

CÆLIA.

What do you mean?

MODELY.

That you make the most sincere of lovers, the happiest of mankind. The addition of your fortune will add splendor to our felicity; and the frowns of disappointed love, only heighten our enjoyments.

CÆLIA.

Oh thou vile one!——How does that cruel generous man who has rejected me, rise on the comparison!

MODELY.

Rejected you?——Sir John Dorilant?

CÆLIA.

Yes, Mr. Modely, that triumph at least is yours. I have offered myself, and been refused. My hand and fortune equally disdained. But may perpetual happiness attend him, where'er his honest, honest heart shall fix!

MODE-

MODELY.

O, madam, your inexperience deceives you. He knows the integrity of your mind, and trusts to that for recompence. His seeming disinterestedness is but the surer method of compleating his utmost wishes.

CÆLIA.

Blasphemer, stop thy tongue. The purity of his intentions is as much above thy malice, as thy imitation.

[*She walks to one side of the stage, and Modely stands disconcerted on the other.*

Enter LADY BEVERLEY.

LADY.

Well, child, what has the man said to thee? Cousin Modely, your servant; you find our plot would not take, they were too quick upon us. —— Hey day! what has been doing here?

MODELY.

O, madam, you are my only refuge; a wretch on the brink of despair flies to you for protection. That amiable creature is in full possession of herself and fortune, and yet rejects my tenderest sollicitations.

LADY.

Really!——What is all this? Tell me, Cælia, has the man actually given up all right and title to thee real and personal? Come, come, I must be a principal actress, I find, in this affair.——Decency and decorum require it.—Tell me, child, is it so?

CÆLIA.

Sir John Dorilant, madam, with a generosity peculiar to himself, (cruel generosity!) has cancelled every obligation which could confine my choice. These

Thefe papers confirm the freedom he has given me
——and rob me of all future comfort.

L A D Y.

Indeed! I did not expect this of him; but I am
heartily glad of it. Give *me* the papers, child.

C Æ L I A.

No, madam!——Ufelefs as they are, they are
yet my own.

L A D Y.

Ufelefs?——What do you mean? **Has the bafe**
man laid any other embargo on thee, child?

C Æ L I A.

I cannot bear, madam, even from you, to hear
Sir John Dorilant treated with difrefpect.————
Ufelefs!——Yes, they fhall be ufelefs. Thus, thus
I tear them into atoms, and difdain a liberty which
but too juftly reproaches *my* conduct. Your advice, madam, has already made me miferable, but
it fhall not make me ungrateful or unjuft.

[*Exit Cælia.*

L A D Y.

I am aftonifhed, I never faw the girl in fuch a
way before. Why this is errant difobedience,
coufin Modely. I muft after her, and know the
bottom of it.—Don't defpair. [*Exit Lady.*

B E L M O U R (coming out of the arbour.)

Come. See, Overcome!——O poor Cæfar!

M O D E L Y (humming a tune.)

You think I am difconcerted now?

B E L M O U R

Why really I fhould think fomething of that
kind.

M O D E L Y.

You never were more miftaken in your life.——
Egad 'tis a fpirited girl. She and Sir John Dorilant were certainly born for one another. I have a
good

good mind to take compaſſion of them, and let them come together. They muſt and ſhall be man and wife, and I will e'en go back to Araminta.

BELMOUR.

Thou haſt a moſt aſtoniſhing aſſurance.

MODELY.

Huſh!——ſhe is coming this way——get into your hole again and be dumb.—Now you ſhall ſee a ſcene of triumph indeed.

BELMOUR.

Have a care, Cæſar, you have the Britons to deal with.   [*Retires.*

Enter ARAMINTA.

ARAMINTA.

What, are they gone? and my wretch here by himſelf?—O that I could diſſemble a little!—I will, if my heart burſts for it.——O, Mr. Modely, I am half aſhamed to ſee you;—but my brother has ſigned thoſe odious writings.

MODELY.

Then thus I ſeize my charmer.

ARAMINTA.

Agreeable raſcal!——Be quiet, can't you, you think one ſo forward now.

MODELY.

I cannot, will not be reſtrained, when the dear object of my wiſhes meets me with kind compliance in her eyes and voice!—To-morrow!——'Tis an age, why ſhould we wait for that? To-night, my angel, to-night may make us one, and the fair proſpect of our halcyon days even from this hour begin.

ARA-

ARAMINTA.

Who would not think this fellow, with his **blank** verse now, was in earneft? But I know him **tho**-roughly.——Indeed Mr. Modely, you are too **pref**-fing, marriage is a ferious thing. Befides, you know, this idle buftle betwixt my brother and Cælia, which you feem to think me ignorant of, and which you, in fome meafure, tho' undefignedly I dare fay, have occafioned, may obftruct us a little.

MODELY.

Not at all, my dear; an amufement *en paffant*; the meer raillery **of** gallantry **on my fide**, to oblige her **impertinent** mother (who, you know, has **a** *penchant* for Sir John herfelf) was the whole infignificant bufinefs. Perhaps, indeed, I was fomething blameable in it.

ARAMINTA.

Why really I think fo, in your fituation. But are you fure it went no farther? nothing elfe paffed **between** you?

MODELY.

Nothing **in** nature.

ARAMINTA.

Dear me, how miftaken people are. I cannot fay that I believed it; but they told me, **that** you had actually propofed to **marry** her, **that the** girl was near confenting, **and that** the **mother** was your friend **in the** affair.

MODELY.

The mere malice, and invention of lady Beverley.

ARAMINTA.

And there is not a word of truth in it then?

MODELY.

Not a fyllable --- You **know** my foul is yours.

K   ARA-

A R A M I N T A.

O thou villain!—I thought to have kept my temper, and to have treated you with the contempt you deserve; but this insolence is intolerable. Can you imagine that I am a stranger to your proceedings? a deaf, blind ideot?—O I could tear this foolish heart, which, cheated by its passion, has encouraged such an insult.—How, how have I deserved this treatment?   [*Bursting into tears.*

M O D E L Y (greatly alarmed.)

By holy faith!—by every power above! you, and you only are the passion of my soul.—May every curse ——

A R A M I N T A.

Away, deceiver—these tears are the tears of resentment. My resolution melts not in my eyes. 'Tis fixed, unalterable! You might imagine from the gayety of my temper, that it had its levity too. But know, Sir, that a woman who has once been duped, defies all future machinations.

M O D E L Y.

Hear me, madam——nay, you shall hear me.—

A R A M I N T A.

Shall!---insufferable insolence!--Go, Sir; for any thing which regards me, you are free as air, free as your licentious principles. Nor shall a thought of what I once esteemed you, disturb my future quiet. There are men who think me not contemptible, and under whose protection I may shelter my disgrace.——Unhand me—this is the last time I shall probably ever see you; and I may tell you in parting, that you have used me cruelly; and that Cælia knows you as perfectly as I do.

[*Exit Araminta.*
M O D E-

MODELY (ſtands confounded.)

Enter BELMOUR.

BELMOUR.

Cæſar aſhamed!——and well he may i'faith. Why, man, what is the matter with you? Quite dumb? quite confounded? Did not I always tell you that you loved her?

MODELY.

I feel it ſenſibly.

BELMOUR.

And I can tell you another ſecret.

MODELY.

What's that?

BELMOUR.

That ſhe loves you.

MODELY.

O that ſhe did!

BELMOUR.

Did!—— Every word, every motion of paſſion through her whole converſation betrayed it involuntarily. I wiſh it had been otherwiſe.

MODELY.

Why?

BELMOUR.

Becauſe I had ſome thoughts of circumventing you. But I find it will be in vain. Therefore purſue her properly, and ſhe is yours.

MODELY.

O never, Belmour, never.—I have ſinned beyond a poſſibility of pardon. That ſhe did love me, I have had a thouſand proofs, which like a brain-

K 2

leſs

lefs ideot I wantonly trifled with. What a piti-
ful rafcal have I made myfelf?

BELMOUR.

Why in that I agree with you; but don't defpair, man; you may ftill be happier than you deferve.

MODELY.

With what face can I approach her? Every circumftance of her former affection, now rifes in
judgment againft me. O Belmour! fhe has
taught me to blufh.

BELMOUR.

And I affure you it becomes you mightily.

MODELY.

Where can I apply?—How can I addrefs her?
All that I can poffibly do, will only look like a
mean artificial method, of patching up my other
difappointment.

BELMOUR.

More miracles ftill! She has not only taught
you to blufh, but has abfolutely made a man of
honour of you!

MODELY.

Raillery is out of feafon.

Enter a SERVANT.

SERVANT.

Mrs. Araminta, Sir, defires to fpeak with you.

MODELY (eagerly.)

With me?

SERVANT.

No, Sir, with Mr. Belmour.

BELMOUR.

With me?

SER-

SERVANT.

Yes, Sir.

BELMOUR.

Where is she?

SERVANT.

In the close walk by the house, Sir.

BELMOUR.

And alone?

SERVANT.

Entirely, Sir.

BELMOUR.

I wait upon her this instant.   [*Exit Servant.*

MODELY.

Belmour, you shall not stir.

BELMOUR.

By my faith but I will, Sir.

MODELY.

She said there were men to whom she could fly
for protection. By my soul she intends to propose
herself to you.

BELMOUR,

And if she does, I shall certainly accept her offer.

MODELY.

I'll cut your thtoat if you do.

BELMOUR.

And do you think to fright me by that? I fancy
I can cut throats as well as other people. Your
servant. If I cannot succeed for myself, I'll speak
a good word for you.   [*Exit Belmour.*

MODELY.

What can this mean?——I am upon thorns till
I know the event. I must watch them. —— No,
that is dishonest. —— Dishonest! How virtuous
does a real passion make one!—— Heigh ho!
                    [*Walks about in disorder.*

He seems in great haste to go to her.   He has
                            turned

turned into the walk already.——That abominable
old fashioned cradle work makes the hedges so
thick, there is no seeing through them.——An
open lawn has ten thousand times the beauty, and
is kept at by less expence by half.————These
cursed unnatural chairs are always in the way too.

[*Stumbling against one of the garden chairs.*]

What a miserable dog am I?——I would give
an arm to know what they are talking about.——
We talk of female coquettes! By my soul we
beat them at their own weapons!——Stay——one
stratagem I may yet put in practice, and it is an
honest one.——The thought was lucky.——I will
about it instantly. Poor Modely!——How has
thy vanity reduced thee?

END of the FOURTH ACT.

ACT V.

SCENE *continues.*

ARAMINTA *and* BELMOUR.

ARAMINTA.

YOU find, Mr. Belmour, that I have seen your partialities, and like a woman of honour I have confessed my own. Your behaviour to your friend is generous beyond comparison, and I could almost join in the little stratagem you propose, merely to see if he deserves it.

BELMOUR.

Indeed, madam, you mistake him utterly: Vanity is his ruling vice; an idle affectation of success among the ladies, which makes fools admire, and boys envy him, is the master passion of his giddy heart. The severe checks he has met with to-day, have sufficiently opened his understanding; and the real possession of one valuable woman, whom he dreads to lose, will soon convince him how despicable his folly has made him.

ARAMINTA.

I am afraid, Mr. Belmour, a man who has half his life been pursuing bubbles, without perceiving their insignificance, will be easily tempted to resume

3   sume

fume the chace. The poffeffion of one reality will hardly convince him that the reft were fhadows. And a woman muft be an ideot indeed, who thinks of fixing a man to herfelf after marriage, whom fhe could not fecure before it. To begin with infenfibility, O fie, Mr. Modely.

BELMOUR.

You need not fear it, madam; his heart ——

ARAMINTA.

Is as idle as our converfation on the fubject. I beg your pardon for the comparifon; as I do, for having fent for you in this manner. But I thought it neceffary that both you and Mr. Modely fhould know my real fentiments, undifguifed by paffion.

BELMOUR.

And may I hope you will concur in my propofal?

ARAMINTA.

I don't know what to fay to it, it is a piece of mummery which I am ill fuited for at prefent. But if an opportunity fhould offer, I muft confefs I have enough of the woman in me, not to be infenfible to the charms of an innocent revenge.——But this other intricate bufinefs, if you can affift me in that, you will oblige me beyond meafure. There are two hearts, Mr. Belmour, worthy to be united! Had my brother a little lefs honour, and fhe a little lefs fenfibility —— But I know not what to think of it.

BELMOUR.

In that, madam, I can certainly affift you.

ARAMINTA.

How, dear Mr. Belmour?

BELMOUR.

I have been a witnefs, unknown to Cælia, to fuch a converfation, as will clear up every doubt Sir John can poffibly have entertained.

ARA-

ARAMINTA.

You charm me when you say so.—— As I live,
here comes my brother. ——— Stay ; is not that
wretch Modely with him ? He is actually. What
can his affurance be plotting now ?—Come this
way, Mr. Belmour ; we will watch them at a dif-
tance, that no harm may happen between them, and
talk to the girl firft ! The monfter !—— *Exeunt*

Enter SIR JOHN DORILANT *and*
MODELY.

MODELY. (Entering and looking after Araminta
and Belmour.)
They are together ftill ! ———
But let me refume my nobler felf.

SIR JOHN.

Why will you follow me, Mr. Modely ? I have
purpofely avoided you.— My heart fwells with indignation. ———I know not what may be the con-
fequence.

MODELY.

Upon my honour, Sir John——

SIR JOHN.

Honour, Mr. Modely ! 'tis a facred word. You
ought to fhudder when you pronounce it. Honour
has no exiftence but in the breaft of truth. 'Tis
the harmonious refult of every virtue combined.—
You have fenfe, you have knowledge; but I can affure you, Mr. Modely, tho' parts and knowledge,
without the dictates of juftice, or the feelings of humanity, may make a bold and mifchievous member
of fociety even courted by the world, they only,
in my eye, make him more contemptible.

MODELY.

This I can bear, Sir John, ——becaufe I have
deferved it.

L   SIR

SIR JOHN.

You may think, perhaps, it is only an idle affair with a lady, what half mankind are guilty of, and what the conceited wits of your acquaintance will treat with raillery. Faith with a woman! ridiculous! — But let me tell you, Mr. Modely, the man who even slightly deceives a believing and a trusting woman, can never be a man of honour.

MODELY.

I own the truth of your assertions. I feel the aweful superiority of your real virtue. Nor should any thing have dragged me into your presence, so much I dreaded it, but the sincerest hope of making you happy.

SIR JOHN.

Making me happy, Mr. Modely! —— You have put it out of your own power.———[*Walks from him, then turns to him again.*] —— You mean, I suppose, by a resignation of Cælia to me.

MODELY.

Not of Cælia only, but her affections.

SIR JOHN.

Vain, and impotent proposal!

MODELY.

Sir John, 'tis not a time for altercation.——— By all my hopes of bliss here and hereafter, you are the real passion of her soul.——— Look not so unbelieving: by heaven 'tis true ; and nothing but an artful insinuation of your never intending to marry her, and even concurring in our affair, could ever have made her listen one moment to me.

SIR JOHN.

Why do I hear you? —— O Mr. Modely, you touch my weakest part.

MODE-

MODELY.

Cherish the tender feelings, and be happy.

SIR JOHN.

Is it possible that amiable creature can think and talk tenderly of me? I know her generosity; but generosity is **not** the point.

MODELY.

Believe me, Sir, 'tis more; 'tis real unaffected passion. Her innocent soul speaks through her eyes the honest dictates of her heart. In our last conference, notwithstanding her mother's commands; notwithstanding, what I blush to own, my utmost ardent solicitations to the contrary, she persisted in her integrity, tore the papers which left her choice free, and treated us with an indignation which added charms to virtue.

SIR JOHN.

O these flattering sounds! —— Would I could believe them!

MODELY.

Belmour, as well as myself, and lady Beverley, was a witness of the truth of them. I thought it my duty to inform you, as I know your delicacy with regard to her. And indeed I would in some measure endeavour to repair the injuries I have offered to your family, before I leave it for ever. ——O Sir John, let not an ill-judged nicety debar you from a happiness, which stands with open arms to receive you. Think what my folly has lost in Araminta; and, when your indignation at the affront is a little respited, be blest yourself, and pity me. —— [*As he goes out, he still looks after Araminta and Belmour.*] —— They are together still; but I will go round that way to the house.

'*Exit* Modely.

SIR

SIR JOHN.

What can this mean?——— He cannot intend
to deceive me ; he feems too fincerely affected. —
I muft, I will believe him. The mind which fufpects injuftice, is half guilty of it itfelf.———Talks
tenderly of me? Tore the parpers? Treated them
with indignation? Heavens! what a flow of tender joy comes over me!—— Shall Cælia then be
mine? How my heart dances! O! I could be
wondrous foolifh!—Well, Jonathan.

Enter STEWARD.

STEWARD.

The gentleman, Sir ——

SIR JOHN.

What of the gentleman? I am ready for any
thing.

STEWARD.

Will wait upon your honour to-morrow, as you
are not at leifure.

SIR JOHN.

With all my heart. Now or then, whenever he
pleafes.

STEWARD.

I am glad to fee your honour in fpirits.

SIR JOHN.

Spirits! Jonathan! I am light as air.—Make a
thoufand excufes to him ; —— but let it be to-
morrow, however, for I fee lady Beverley coming
this way.

STEWARD.

Heaven blefs his good foul! I love to fee him
merry.   [*Exit.*

Enter

Enter LADY BEVERLEY.

LADY.

If I don't interrupt you, Sir John ——

SIR JOHN.

Interrupt me, madam? 'tis impoſſible.

LADY.

For I would not be guilty of an indecorum, even to you.

SIR JOHN.

Come, come, lady Beverley, theſe little bickerings muſt be laid aſide. Give me your hand, lady. Now we are friends [*Kiſſing it.*] —— How does your lovely daughter?

LADY.

You are in mighty good humour, Sir John; perhaps every body may not be ſo.

SIR JOHN.

Every body muſt be ſo, madam, where I come; I am joy itſelf.

"The jolly god that leads the jocund hours!"

LADY.

What is come to the man? —— Whatever it is, I ſhall damp it preſently. —— [*Aſide.*] ——
Do you chuſe to hear what I have to ſay, Sir John?

SIR JOHN.

You can ſay nothing, madam, but that you conſent, and Cælia is my own. —— Yes, you yourſelf have been a witneſs to her integrity. Come, indulge me, lady Beverley. Declare it all, and let me liſten to my happineſs.

LADY.

I ſhall declare nothing, Sir John, on that ſubject: what I have to ſay is of a very different import. —— In ſhort, without circumlocution, or

4

any unnecessary embarrassment to entangle the affair, I and my daughter are of an opinion, that it is by no means proper for us to continue any longer in your family.

SIR JOHN.

Madam!

LADY.

This is what I had to declare, Sir John.

SIR JOHN.

Does Cælia, madam, desire to leave me?

LADY.

It was a proposal of her own.

SIR JOHN.

Confusion!

LADY.

And a very sensible one too, in my opinion. For when people are not so easy together, as might be expected, I know no better remedy than parting.

SIR JOHN. (Aside.)

Sure, this is no trick of Modely's, to get her away from me?—He talked too himself, of leaving my family immediately.—I shall relapse again.

LADY.

I find, Sir John, you are somewhat disconcerted: but, for my part —

SIR JOHN.

O torture!

LADY.

I say, for my part, Sir John, it might have been altogether as well, perhaps, if we had never met.

SIR JOHN.

I am sorry, madam, my behaviour has offended you, but ———.

Enter

Enter ARAMINTA, CÆLIA, *and* BELMOUR.

ARAMINTA. (to Cælia as she enters.)

Leave the house indeed! Come, come, you shall speak to him.——— What is all this disorder for? Pray, brother, has any thing new happened?—— That wretch has been before-hand with us—(*Aside to Belmour.*)

LADY.

Nothing at all, Mrs. Araminta; I have only made a very reasonable proposal to him, which he is pleased to treat with his and your usual incivility.

SIR JOHN.

You wrong us, madam, with the imputation.——(*After a pause, and some irresolution, he goes up to Cælia.*)—— I thought, Miss Beverley, I had already given up my authority, and that you were perfectly at liberty to follow your own inclinations. I could have wished, indeed, to have still assisted you with my advice; and I flattered myself that my presence would have been no restraint upon your conduct. But I find it is otherwise. My very roof is grown irksome to you, and the innocent pleasure I received in observing your growing virtues, is no longer to be indulged to me.

CÆLIA.

O Sir, put not so hard a construction upon what I thought a blameless proceeding. Can it be wondered at, that I should fly from him, who has twice rejected me with disdain?

SIR JOHN.

With disdain, Cælia?

CÆLIA.

C Æ L I A.

Who has withdrawn from me even his parental tendernefs, and driven me to the hard neceffity of avoiding him, left I fhould offend him farther.

I know how much my inexperience wants a faithful guide ; I know what cruel cenfures a malicious world will pafs upon my conduct; but I muft bear them all. For he who might protect me from myfelf, protect me from the infults of licentious tongues, abandons me to fortune.

SIR JOHN.

O Cælia !—have I, have I abandoned thee ?——Heaven knows my inmoft foul how it did rejoice but a few moments ago, when Modely told me that your heart was mine !

ARAMINTA.

Modely !—— Did Modely tell you fo ? —— Do you hear that, Mr. Belmour ?

SIR JOHN.

He did, my fifter, with every circumftance which could increafe his own guilt, and her integrity.

ARAMINTA.

That was honeft, however.

SIR JOHN.

I thought it fo, and refpected him accordingly. O he breathed comfort to a defpairing wretch ! but now a thoufand thoufand doubts crowd in upon me. He leaves my houfe this inftant; nay, may be gone already. Cælia too is flying from me,—— perhaps to join him, and with her happier lover, fmile at my undoing !—— (Leans on Araminta.)

C Æ L I A.

I burft with indignation!—— Can I be fufpected of

of such treachery? Can you, Sir, who know my
every thought, harbour such a suspicion?—O madam, this contempt have you brought upon me.
A want of deceit was all the little negative praise I
had to boast of, and that is now denied me.

[Leans on Lady Beverley.

LADY.

Come away, child.

CÆLIA.

No, madam. I have a harder task still to per-
form.   *[Comes up to Sir John.*
To offer you my hand again under these circumstances, thus despicable as you have made me, may
seem an insult. But I mean it not as such.—O Sir, if
you ever loved my father, in pity to my orphan state,
let me not leave you. Shield me from the world,
shield me from the worst of misfortunes, your own
unkind suspicions.

ARAMINTA.

What fooling is here? Help me, Mr. Belmour.
——There, take her hand. —— And now let it
go if you can.

SIR JOHN *(grasping her hand.)*

O Cælia! may I believe Modely? Is your heart
mine?

CÆLIA.

It is, and ever shall be.

SIR JOHN.

Transporting extacy!——   *[Turning to Cælia.*

LADY.

I should think Sir John, a mother's consent——
tho' Mrs. Araminta, I see, has been so very good to
take that office upon herself.

M   SIR

SIR JOHN.

I beg your pardon, madam; my thoughts were too much engaged. —— But may I hope for your concurrence?

LADY.

I don't know what to fay to you; I think you have bewitch'd the girl amongft you.

ARAMINTA.

Indeed, lady Beverley, this is quite prepofterous. ——Ha! —— He here again! —— Protect me, Mr. Belmour.

Enter MODELY.

MODELY.

Madam, you need fly no where for protection: you have no infolence to fear from me. I am humbled fufficiently, and the poft-chaife is now at the door to banifh me for ever. — My fole bufinefs here is, to unite that virtuous man with the moft worthy of her fex.

ARAMINTA (half afide.)

Thank you for the compliment —— Now, Mr. Belmour.

LADY.

You may fpare yourfelf that trouble, coufin Modely; the girl is irrecoverably gone already.

MODELY.

May all the happinefs they deferve attend them!

      [*Going, then looks back at Araminta.*
I cannot leave her.

SIR JOHN.

Mr. Modely, is there nobody here befides, whom you ought to take leave of?

MODE-

MODELY.

I own my parting from that lady (*to Araminta*) should not be in silence; but a conviction of my guilt stops my tongue from utterance.

ARAMINTA.

I cannot say I quite believe that; but as our affair may make some noise in the world, for the sake of my own character, I must beg of you to declare before this company, whether any part of my conduct has given even a shadow of excuse for the insult I have received. If it has, be honest, and proclaim it.

MODELY.

None by heaven; the crime was all my own, and I suffer for it justly and severely —— with shame I speak it, notwithstanding the appearances to the contrary, my heart was ever yours, and ever will be.

ARAMINTA.

I am satisfied; and will honestly confess, the sole reason of my present appeal was this, that where I had destined my hand, my conduct might appear unblemished.   [*Gives her hand to Belmour.*

MODELY.

Confusion! —— then my suspicions were just.

SIR JOHN.

Sister!

CÆLIA.

Araminta!

ARAMINTA.

What do ye mean? What are ye surprized at? —— The insinuating Mr. Modely can never want mistresses any where. Can he, Mr. Belmour? You know him perfectly.

M 2   MODE-

M O D E L Y.

Diftraction!——Knows me? Yes, he does know me. The villain! though he triumphs in my fufferings, knows what I feel!——You, madam, are juft in your feverity, from you I have deferved every thing; the anguifh, the defpair which muft attend my future life comes from you like heaven's avenging minifter!——But for him——

[Sir John interpofes.

O for a fword!——But I fhall find a time, and a fevere one.——Let me go, Sir John——

A R A M I N T A.

I'll carry on the farce no longer.——Rafh inconfiderate madman! The fword which pierces Mr. Belmour's breaft, would rob you of the beft of friends.——This pretended marriage, for it is no more, was merely contrived by him, to convince me of your fincerity.——Embrace him as your guardian angel, and learn from him to be virtuous.

B E L M O U R.

O madam, let me ftill plead for him. Surely when a vain man feels himfelf in the wrong, you cannot defire him to fuffer a greater punifhment.

A R A M I N T A.

I have done with fooling.—— You told me today, lady Beverley, that he would never return to me.

L A D Y.

And I told you at the fame time, madam, that if he did—you would take him.

A R A M I N T A.

In both you were miftaken.——Mr. Modely, your laft behaviour to Cælia and my brother, fhews a generofity of temper I did not think you capable

of,

of, and for that I thank you. But to be serious on our own affair, whatever appearance your present change may carry with it, your transactions of to-day have been such, that I can never hereafter have that respect for you, which a wife ought to have for her husband.

SIR JOHN

I am sorry to say it, Mr. Modely, her determination is, I fear, too just. Trust to time however, at least let us part friends, and not abruptly. We should conceal the failings of each other, and if it must come to that, endeavour to find out specious reasons for breaking off the match, without injuring either party.

ARAMINTA.

To shew how willing I am to conceal every thing, now I have had my little female revenge, as my brother has promised us the fiddles this evening, Mr. Modely, as usual, shall be my partner in the dance.

MODELY.

I have deserved this ridicule, madam, and am humbled to what you please.

ARAMINTA.

Why then, brother, as we all seem in a strange dilemma, why may'nt we have one dance in the garden? it will put us in good humour.

SIR JOHN.

As you please, madam.—Call the fiddles hither. —Don't despair Mr. Modely. [*Exit Sir John.*

LADY.

I will not dance, positively.

BELMOUR.

Indeed but you shall, madam; do you think I will be the only disconsolate swain without a partner? Besides, you see there are two that we muſt call in the butler and the ladies maids even to help out the figure.

SIR JOHN.

Come, lady Beverley, you muſt lay aſide all animoſities. If I have behaved improperly to you to-day, I moſt ſincerely aſk your pardon, and hope the anxieties I have been under will ſufficiently plead my excuſe ; my future conduct ſhall be irreproachable. [*Turning to Cælia.*

Here have I placed my happineſs, and here expect it. O Cælia, if the ſeriouſneſs of my behaviour ſhould hereafter offend you, impute it to my infirmity ; it can never proceed from want of affection.

> A heart like mine its *own* diſtreſs contrives,
> And feels *moſt* ſenſibly the pain it gives ;
> Then even its frailties candidly approve,
> For, if it errs, it errs from too much love.

A DANCE.

EPILOGUE.

Spoken **before** the DANCE,

By Mrs. YATES and Mr. PALMER, in the
Characters of ARAMINTA and MODELY.

ARAMINTA.

*W*ELL, *ladies, am I right, or am I not ?*
    Should not this foolish passion be forgot ;
This fluttering something, scarce to be exprest,
Which pleads for coxcombs in each female breast ?
How mortified he look'd ! — and looks so still.

                [Turning to Modely.

He really may repent —— perhaps he will. ——

MODELY.

Will, Araminta ? —— Ladies, be so good,
Man's made of frail materials, flesh and blood.
We all offend at some unhappy crisis,
Have whims, caprices, vanities, — and vices.
Your happier sex by nature was design'd,
Her last best work, to perfect humankind.
No spot, no blemish the fair frame deforms,
No avarice taints, no naughty passion warms
Your firmer hearts. No love of change in you
E'er taught desire to stray. ——

ARAMINTA.

All this is true.

Yet

EPILOGUE.

Yet stay ; the men, perchance, will call it sneer,
And some few ladies think you not sincere.
For your petition, whether wrong or right,
Whate'er it be, withdraw it for to-night.
Another time, if I should want a spouse,
I may myself report it to the house :
At present, let us strive to mend the age ;
Let justice reign, at least upon the stage.
Where the fair dames, who like to live by rule,
May learn two lessons from the LOVER'S SCHOOL
While Cælia's choice instructs them how to chuse,
And my refusal warns them to refuse.

THE END.

ERRATA.